The Christmas ABC

By Florence Johnson • Illustrated by Eloise Wilkin

 A GOLDEN BOOK • NEW YORK

A
is for Angels
   looking down from above,
Guardians of Heaven
   that sing of God's love.

B is for Bells
    that ring in the steeple,
Bearing glad tidings
    to us and all people.

C is for Christmas,
    a most joyful day.
We celebrate Jesus
    in his warm bed of hay.

D is for Dancer

and the sleigh full of toys

That Santa will bring

to good girls and boys.

E is for Evergreen,
    so pretty to see
When it's all dressed up
    as a fine Christmas tree.

F is for Flower,
   bright as the star
That shepherds and
   Wise Men saw from afar.

G is for Giving
   of gifts to each other.
A package for Daddy
   and something for Mother,
And let's give a present to
   some girl or boy
Who surely would like
   a nice Christmas toy.

H is for Holly
with berries so red
To please little children
wherever it's spread.

I is for Icicles
that shine in the sun
And ice on the pond
where skaters have fun.

 is for Jesus,
    Who was born Christmas Day,
The baby God sent us
    to teach us His way.

K is for Kitten,
　　so warm and so cozy
When Santa comes in,
　　so jolly and rosy.

L is for Lamp that glows
　　oh so bright,
A welcome to those
　　who pass in the night.

M is for Mailbox
the postman will fill
With letters and cards,
all bearing Good Will.

N is for Neighbors
who come over to say,
"Merry Christmas to all,
what a joyous day!"

is for Ornaments
that glitter so bright
And make Christmas trees
a most beautiful sight.

is for Plum Pudding,
a fine Christmas treat.
There'll be cranberries, turkey,
and nice things to eat.

is for Quiet,
not even a peep,
For Santa is waiting
till all are asleep.

R is for Ribbon.

Tying bows
is such fun!

Christmas gifts look so pretty
when wrapping is done.

is for Santa Claus,

Stockings and Sleigh,

And all of the things

that make Christmas Day gay.

For Santa
will come Christmas Eve,
we all know,

To fill all our stockings right down to the toe.

T is for Trees
   full of tinsel and lights.
Surely they're one
   of our Christmas delights.

is for Underwear,
　　red flannel, you know,
To keep Santa warm
　　from his head to his toe.
Back home at the Pole
　　with his feet near the fire,
He wears his red flannels
　　till it's time to retire.

V is for Voices
of boys in the choir,
Singing God's praises
in festive attire.

Sing of a manger, oh, sing of the glory,

W is for Wreath
   that we hang on the door,
Like a crown for the King
   little children adore.

 is for Kisses
  when you write someone a letter,
So send a few to Santa Claus
  to say you love him better.

Y is for Yuletide,
    the time for good cheer,
When Santa and presents
    and stockings appear.

Z

is for Zooming
 way up in the sky.
Santa Claus and his reindeer
 now bid you good-bye.